MW00903688

ALPHA BILLIONAIRE ROMANCE

BROKEN PURITY BOOK TWO

By Bridget Taylor

© 2016

Just go to
www.BridgetTaylor.Info to sign
up

*EXCLUSIVE UPDATES

*FREE BOOKS

*NEW REALEASE
ANNOUCEMENTS BEFORE
ANYONE ELSE   GETS THEM

*DISCOUNTS

*GIVEAWAYS

FOR NOTIFACTIONS OF MY
NEW RELEASES :

Never miss my next FREE
PROMO, my next NEW RELEASE
or a GIVEAWAY!

COPYRIGHT

Broken Innocence (Alpha Billionaire Romance Series Book 1)

By Bridget Taylor

Copyright @2015 by Bridget Taylor.

All Rights Reserved.

This book may not be used or reproduced in any form, in whole or in part, without permission from the author or publisher. Any resemblance to actual events, locales or persons whether living or dead is entirely coincidental. This book contains mature content of sexually explicit scenes, situations for adults 18+. Every character in this book is 18+ years of age.

All the characters in this book are fictional

TABLE OF CONTENTS

ONE

I walked past the swamp of reporters in the lobby of the Lennox Building and made my way to the elevators. The cacophony of their voices as they murmured and shared questions drowned out the relaxing sound of the enormous fountain. I smiled to myself, knowing that I really should not take so much joy in this. I turned to look at the reporters and photographers. One of them spotted me and then turned back to her partner to watch the Bluepointe Lounge. I just shook my head. Their mystery girl was standing right there, and none of them saw her.

I was beneath their notice, especially compared to the angelic creatures that populated Lennox Enterprises, beautiful women for Henry Lennox to adore and seduce. As the elevator doors opened behind me, the throng of reports jumped excitedly and began to shout. Ana walked out of the Bluepointe Lounge and began to make her way through the press of people.

I stepped into the elevator and held the *door open* button as others joined me. Ana squeezed past the last of the reporters and dashed to join us. I released the button and offered her a smile.

"Slow news day?" I hoped a little levity would help her. She looked aggravated by the assault.

Ana looked at me evenly and then smiled. "Apparently." She sighed. "Did you enjoy your long weekend?"

I shrugged my shoulders. "The extra day off is always nice."

In truth, I hated it. I spent the day alone, cleaning my apartment. I still had the diamond necklace that Henry gave to me sitting on my dresser. As much as it pained me to look at it, I could not put it away. That seemed like a finality to me, an end. I thought about his words, *when it is done, I hope that you will reconsider things.* Oh how I wanted all of this to be done.

"I hid in my house with a megaphone and told reporters if they did not get off of my lawn that I would shoot them." One of the other girls in the elevator giggled, and I noticed that Ana seemed to brighten at the sound. "My neighbor asked me this morning if I had taken to aging over the weekend."

"It can't last much longer, can it?" I wanted her to say that it would be over soon.

Ana shook her head. "Ternion Communications has been looking for a chink in Mr. Lennox's armor for years. Our media arm is a direct competitor, and we have slowly been gaining traction in Cable and online media."

"Actually," one of the other young women spoke up. I did not recognize her, so I thought she must be from another floor, "we're out performing Ternion in online media. Our Lennox News Online has more subscribers and we are receiving about fifty percent more hits per day."

Ana nodded. "These are the things I miss." Ana gave me another smile as the elevator stopped for the first floor. I looked out to see Lennox Communications on the wall, and the young woman who spoke up and three others stepped off the elevator. We ascended again, stopping at two more floors to let the rest of our co-passengers disembark.

When the doors closed, Ana leaned against one wall and looked at me. "Your co-workers are worried about you."

I felt my blood run cold. Why was my team going to Ana about me? I was performing well, active in each meeting and brainstorming session. Our first campaign with me on the team was a success; the client loved everything that we put together.

"Nothing bad," Ana said. "You have been throwing yourself into your work and you have not been cheerful. They were worried that it had to do with the whole media circus, so they asked me to give you reassurances."

The elevator door opened for our floor. I decided to follow Ana, sensing that our conversation was not finished. When we arrived to her office, she gestured for me to sit down and took her own chair.

"I know that you ended things with Henry. I also understand why." Ana let out an exasperated sigh. "Believe me, I do. It is so much easier to deflect questions about their 'mystery girl' when I point out that she's not been seen with him in two weeks."

I smiled. At least it did something. I imagined an even thicker throng of reporters if they were still spotting me out with him.

"The circus will get better. It is already lessening. I am seeing less mention of it on news segments. Even Ternion is easing up. They will probably be the last sharks to leave. Then life can get back to normal." Ana leaned forward and placed her elbows on her desk. "You need to focus on you. You've lost weight since this all started. You are still letting it take a toll on you."

"I know. I –" I struggled with what to say. I hardly knew Ana. Did I want to confide my emotional turmoil in her?

"Henry is an addictive person," Ana said. "It's fine to miss him, but you still have you and your life. I do not want to see you burn yourself out because of this. If I have to, I will make you join the gym and yoga classes down stairs. You need to let yourself relax and let go."

Ana was right. I thought of the necklace at home. I had to let him go to preserve him. I needed to let my feelings go to preserve me as well.

"Thank you." I seemed to say that a lot to Ana.

"You're welcome. Now get to your office. Nora will be waiting."

I stood. "Yes, ma'am."

I turned and walked out of her office. I crossed through the elevator lobby and up the stairs to the second level of the suite. In the office, the team waited at the planning table. I dropped my purse at my desk and walked over with apologies for my tardiness. Nora waved it off and started the morning planning session. We were being given a second project to work on, and this client was extremely meticulous.

I listened through Nora's debriefing and she handed each of us a folder with pictures from the fashion photo shoots and the instructions from the client. I glanced over it and winced. When she said "meticulous," she apparently meant anal-retentive. I shook my head at the sheer detail in the notes, wondering exactly how we were supposed to get creative with this. It seemed that the client already had a proposal written. We would be doing little more than parroting his ideas back to him.

"I've worked on one other project for Mr. Braedon," Nora said. "He is exacting, but he does appreciate a job well done. I have absolute confidence in all of you."

I looked around at the rest of the team. No one else seemed buoyed by her vote of confidence either. Nora left us to our creative planning and returned to her desk. I began laying out photos and notes, wondering how to turn all of this into something spectacular. His notes were exhaustive. He left little room for interpretation.

"You're doing it again," Michelle whispered, drawing me out of my thoughts. I looked up at her. Around me, everyone had the same serious and concerned look.

"You've been like this forever now," Tina said. "We're worried about you."

"I know," I said. "I talked to Ana this morning, and I appreciate the concern. I just need time."

"The media attention will stop," Lillian said. "It's not like they have found out who you are."

They did not realize, and I smiled in spite of my own feelings.

"I'm not seeing him anymore." I kept my voice low. I was greeted by startled looks from around the table. I held up my hand before anyone could say anything. "I broke everything off. I did not want to make things worse for Henry. I couldn't."

Michelle pouted and looked on the verge of tears.

Tina placed her hand on my shoulder. "You didn't have to do that. It's not like anyone in this building is going to blab to the media. The moment we do, it opens all kinds of floodgates. No one wants to see their face all over the news."

Lillian slapped Tina lightly on the shoulder. "Hello."

Tina frowned at her.

"It's okay," I said. "I didn't think about it like that. I didn't realize just how disciplined the office was."

Lillian glared at Tina and then turned to me, her expression turning gentle. "We all look out for each other, even when we say stupid things to people who do have their faces all over the news."

I laughed as Tina rolled her eyes. "It's okay. It really is. I will be okay too. I'm just getting over having to do what I did."

"You are so strong," Michelle said.

I wished I felt it, but I offered her the best "strong" smile I could. I turned my attention back to the pictures and notes, inviting my teammates to join me in contemplation this time. I wanted to find a pattern, something we could take and twist. I had a feeling that everyone simply regurgitated his ideas back to him. What if we offered him something original?

TWO

By midweek, we had solid ideas for the Braedon project. We would have a proposal together within two weeks easily, and I was confident the client would like it. Our other project was simpler, the client more willing to work with us on ideas. Work was going well, and it was leaving me more time for contemplation. Even though I put the necklace away in a jewelry box, I could not escape the feeling of longing. I missed Henry and had no idea when that would ease.

Another thought came to my mind – Michael. Henry's promise to "take care of this whole mess" still haunted me. I had no idea what a man like him would do. I knew his darkness stretched deep. Would he try to hurt Michael or threaten him? I wanted to reach out to him; I still had his cell number in my phone's contact list, put there in case I needed to reach him for an emergency. I had no idea what I would say to him. "Henry had said something that could be a threat, but might not be." I had a feeling that would just add more fuel to the fire.

As I walked into the Lennox Advertising offices on Friday, I felt good about work, confused about Michael, and depressed about Henry. I made my way up the stairway and paused, hearing his voice. I did not hear what he said, but a giggle followed it. I looked down to see him pass by the stairway, and attractive blonde walking with him, blushing at something that he said. I rolled my eyes and finished my ascent up the stairs.

My depression was starting to shift into something else.

After our morning brainstorming session, I decided that some hot tea was in order. I made my way to the break room and paused at the doorway. Two women were talking inside, and their conversation made me hesitant to enter.

"Nipple clamps?" One sounded astounded. I could not place a name to the voice and hated that I knew so few people here.

"Yes. Hard too. Then he kept thumping them. It drove me crazy," the other said.

"Sounds like you had a hard night."

I turned to walk back to the office. Tea could wait. I thought I might enjoy something a little stronger at lunch anyway. It seemed that Henry had decided to move on. I pulled my phone from my pocket and flipped through until I found Michael's number. I selected text message.

Busy this weekend?

I walked into the office and to my desk. I needed to work on projects. I started going over notes and designs as my phone buzzed.

I'm surprised to hear from you. I'm not busy.

I smiled.

Coffee Sunday?

I continued working on notes. Michael's message came back, *sure*. I sent him a time and location and put my phone away. I would be able to make sure that he was okay. I told myself that was all that it was, and not some immature ploy to "move on" myself.

I decided to spend my Friday and Saturday out with friends from college. It allowed me to put work and the drama tied to it out of my mind. It was also nice simply to be young again, not a woman chasing a career, but a young woman just enjoying life. I could be that girl again, whose biggest worry was getting a homework assignment in on time, not if the paparazzi was going to show up on her doorstep.

That my friends had not pieced together that I was the "mysterious woman" on Henry Lennox's arm did not surprise me. I was the girl who studied hard all week and let her hair down on the weekend. I was not the kind of person who would accompany a playboy to a show. I also noticed that most of them simply did not care. The news was big to people like my mother, who watched Henry Lennox rise through the media ranks like a rocket ship. For my friends, there was always a Henry Lennox, and rich people always got into trouble.

It was refreshing to be in a crowd that was not concerned with what was happening among the elite of society. We were just kids again, hopping between clubs and enjoying the simplest part of life. We were having fun.

By Sunday, I was calm and ready to meet with Michael. I arrived early to the Starbucks I told him to meet me at, ordered my Chai Latte, and sat down at a table. He joined me a few minutes after five, with his own purchased coffee in hand. He looked casual in blue jeans and a button down shirt. His brown hair was combed back neatly and his face was clean-shaven. In my mind, I had expected to see the stereotypical unemployed job seeker, sweatpants, t-shirt, and eternal five o'clock shadow. It seemed that he too was moving on.

Except for the whole lawsuit thing, of course.

"You're looking well," Michael said as he sat down. He offered me a relaxed smile. I saw something in his eyes, but I was not sure just what to make of it. It was curiosity and something else. "I was not really expecting you to message me, all things considered."

"You left suddenly," I said. "I wanted to make sure that everything was okay."

That something else in his eyes became more prominent. It made me think of the exchanged glances before our conversation. I was not sure what to make of Michael. He seemed attracted to me, interested. If he was, then why push me to Henry?

"I'm sorry that you got mixed up in everything." Michael sipped his coffee. "It wasn't my intention."

"What did you expect would happen?" I said it harsher than I meant to, but the point had to be made. "You named me in the complaint. You practically pointed at Henry and said 'if you want your place on the project, you need to sleep with him.'"

Michael almost choked on his sip of coffee. He coughed a few times and shook his head. "You didn't have to do that. I only meant for you not to give him the cold shoulder."

I glared at Michael. Innocent was not the same as stupid, but he did not seem to be getting it.

"I didn't mean for you to get played by him." Michael was still trying to recover.

I picked up my own drink. "Henry wasn't playing me."

Michael sat back. "That's what men like Henry do. It's all they know how to do."

I shrugged my shoulders and tried to ignore the jealousy that I saw in Michael's eyes as he spoke. It was hard to tell if he was jealous of Henry in general or jealous over me. I did not want to chase it right now. I was willing to accept that Michael did not mean for me to be hurt or pulled into a media whirlwind. I did not buy his back peddling, however. I wished that he would just be honest with me about his intentions.

I decided to change the subject to something else. I was not there to talk to him about the past. I was there to make sure that he was okay. I asked what he was doing now, and learned he was working with Lellman& White. I was not sure what to make of that. There were dozens of other advertising agencies in town who would be happy to hire a midlevel executive fresh from Lennox Advertising. Then I remembered that Lellman& White had been bought out by Ternion Communications about three years ago. I wondered if they smelled a controversy when they saw Michael on the market or just hoped for inside information. In either case, the thought that Michael was just a pawn in a larger game softened me to his situation.

"So, I have a question." We had been talking for over an hour, sipping our drinks as they slowly cooled.

He was moving on, but I still did not have an answer to my main question coming here. "This lawsuit, do you ever worry about going after someone like Henry Lennox?"

Michael laughed and shook his head. "It's intimidating, sure. He's a media giant. Henry may be a womanizer of the worst kind, but when it comes to business, he has a set of principles. They are strange principles, but they are his and he follows them to the letter. At the end of the day, this is all just business."

I nodded. Michael moved on to talking about other things, not even blinking at my question. I felt a sense of relief and shame. Had I allowed the image of Henry Lennox to cloud my judgment of the man? In the end, it really did not matter. For now, at least, Henry was behind me. I focused on the conversation until I decided it was about time to go home. The sun was down and clouds were in the sky. I wanted to get home before the rain started.

Michael walked me to my car to finish off our conversation. I unlocked my door and as I turned to say goodbye to him, he kissed me. His lips touched mine, passionate and firm, and my questions about his attraction were answered. When he pulled away, he smiled.

"Drive careful on your way home." With that, he turned and walked to his own car.

I got into my car and sat down, feeling excited and dizzy from the kiss. My own attraction to Michael leapt up, and I breathed in and out slowly. Michael was the kind of man I could fall for so easily. Even with those feelings stirring, I still could not get Henry out of my mind. I started the engine and pulled out of the parking space slowly. I was going to have to find some way to resolve this, for my sanity's sake at least.

I pulled into the parking lot of my apartment building, finding a space near my apartment and cut the engine. I felt strange. It was more than just the kiss from Michael and my unsettled feelings for Henry. I had this feeling, as though someone were following me. I played back through my drive. I remembered the car Michael walked to, and I did not think I saw it on the drive home.

I stepped out of my car and looked around cautiously. Michael's car was not here. Were there other cars that I did not recognize? I spotted one, a black sedan with a person seated behind the wheel. This, I thought, was the source of the feeling.

The occupant could be anyone, from a private investigator to a mad man. I thought more likely it was a reporter, someone who finally managed to sniff out who I was. Did someone from college finally take notice and recognize me? Had Michael decided to disclose my identity? The thought that he would do something so invasive and then kiss me in the parking lot seemed counter intuitive. It was also not out of keeping for his character.

Placing my keys between my fingers, I walked up to the car slowly. If this were some pervert, I would be ready. If this was a reporter, I would give him a piece of my mind. The driver's side window lowered, and Henry looked up at me. I stepped back, not sure what I should do.

"Are you following me?" I looked around to see if there was anyone else in the parking lot, someone who might call for help if he jumped out of the car.

"Tonight, I was," Henry said. "By chance."

He did not sound convincing, and I did not believe his words.

"You're spying on me." My fear gave way to indignation. How dare he spy on me and invade my privacy.

Henry let out a long sigh. "It's not like that. It's not something I can really explain out here. Can I come inside?"

My heart leapt to a yes, but I hesitated. Everything screamed that I should just turn around and walk inside now. I studied Henry carefully. He looked forlorn and as lost as I felt. I sighed. Henry would not hurt me any more than he would hurt Michael. "Come in."

Henry opened the door and stepped out of his car slowly. I walked to my apartment, not waiting for him to follow and knowing he was right behind me. I opened the door and let him in as the first drops of rain started to fall.

Inside, my apartment felt small and cramped while the world between Henry and I felt enormous. He stood silent in my living room and looked at me, his eyes full of me. I wanted to run to him and hold him, and felt unsure. I realized that I did not even know what I was to him – a conquest, a girlfriend, or just a friend he could play with. I did not know where I stood, and I did not understand why he looked so pained.

"I miss you." He spoke the words as if he had more to say. I thought of the office, of the giggling girl and the overheard conversation.

"If you miss me, why bother with other women?" I asked. I felt silly. I had no claim over him, but the question seemed right to ask. He could not be a jilted lover and a playboy at the same time. He had to choose.

"Why did you have coffee with Michael?"

I frowned. "You are spying on me."

Henry shrugged his shoulders. "I've been watching out for you, to make sure that reporters stay away from you. This has been hard enough on you without having your name and every detail of your life in the papers."

"Someone told you I was having coffee with him and you decided you would, what? Waltz in and break it up?"

Henry placed his hands into the pocket of his pants. "I was making sure you were okay."

I leaned against the back of my couch. "I was making sure he was okay. When we talked about it, you sounded," I struggled for the right words. I thought about him just showing up in my parking lot, sending people to watch me. It was best, I thought, to let him see exactly what it looked like from outside of his grand tower. "You sounded like you wanted to hurt someone."

I braced myself. Henry stared at me and then laughed. His shoulders relaxed, and he seemed to actually be feeling the amusement behind the sound. When he stopped, he fixed me with another serious look.

"I wouldn't harm Michael. I know how it sounded. I guess I know how all of this looks to you. I know people. I have contacts that are helping me control the media storm. When I said that I would take care of it, I just meant that I would get things quiet again, and keep the media from finding you, that's all."

I stared at Henry, trying to sort him out. I had two men in my life, and I was not certain that either one was good for me. One was a manipulator. Even if I believed his good intentions, he turned too easily. The other – I realized I had no idea what Henry was.

"The girls," he continued. "They were a way to try to get past you, to get over you leaving."

"Did it work?" I asked.

Henry shrugged his shoulders. "The media storm is starting to die down, slowly. They've moved from my condo to my office, hoping that some employee will talk to them. No one does. I noticed fewer on Friday. I won't be surprised if the number continues to trickle down this week."

I felt a twinge in my chest. Did he not pick up on the jealousy? Did it not occur to him someone could feel that way about him? He was being adorable, and I thought as I watched him that he had no idea how. "I meant the girls."

Henry took a step forward, shortening the divide between us. "I followed you from the coffee shop to your apartment." He took another step closer to me. "I think I wanted you to see me. I wanted you to challenge me. You have from the moment I saw you. You don't just smile coyly and follow along. You want a reason, a purpose."

To hell with misery and worry. I pushed myself off the couch and threw my arms around him, bringing my lips to his, and kissing him. He brought one arm around my waist and the other to the back of my head, wrapping his fingers in my hair, gripping and pulling as he held me against him and pushed his tongue between my lips. This was what I wanted.

We broke the kiss and Henry pulled my head back by my hair. I gasped at the pain of the pull and he kissed my neck down to my shoulder blade. My body was on fire for wanting him. I brought my hands up to his shirt and began to unbutton it, my fingers sliding down the soft cotton. Beneath, his skin was hot and smooth and I wanted to feel this pressed against me.

He released my hair gently and brought my shirt over my head, discarding it on the couch behind me. My stomach twitched as he moved his fingers down to my jeans to unfasten them and moved to his knees. He pushed down my jeans and panties in one motion and his mouth was there, between my legs hungry and eager to taste me. His lips sucked at me, his tongue danced over my clit, and I cried out. My want, my weeks of denial swelled up into an orgasm and I laced my fingers through his hair, relishing the feel of it.

He did not stop, and my head began to spin and hum with the pleasure he was bringing me. He brought my legs up, one at a time, out of my pants. He draped one leg over his shoulder, opening me wider for him. His hands came up, exploring my body. Fingers pressed inside me as others slid back. I gasped as he teased and danced around the tender hole behind me. I wanted to give him all of me, that as well. As he eased his finger inside, I let out another cry and clenched my fingers, pulling his hair. He sucked harder in response, taking my pleasure from my body as it swelled up again.

His ministrations eased. Henry pulled his fingers from me. I loosened my grip on his hair and looked down as he kissed me softly and lowered my leg. He sat back and looked up at me, his eyes still full of lust. "I want to tie you down to your bed."

In his eyes, I saw the darkness stir. Mixed with his longing, I saw something deeper there. Yes, the bondage was about control, but the control had a purpose. He could not control if I walked out of his life or back into it. In the moment I let him tie me up, however, he could. In that moment, all power was given to him if I stayed or if I left.

"I have scarves in my dresser," I said.

Henry stood. He took my hand and led me back to my bedroom. I opened the dresser and pulled out a pile of soft, satin scarves. Most of them had never been worn. I bought them on impulse, just liking the look and feel of them. He chose one and brought it up to my eyes. I smiled as he wrapped it around my head and tied it gently at the side.

He guided me to lie down and brought my hands and feet out above and below my body. Shivers ran down my spine as the smooth material of the scarves danced across my skin, first my left wrist, and then my right. He tied my ankles and pulled the scarves tight to the foot of my bed. I pulled against my bonds and could not move. I could not see Henry, but I could hear his breathing. I heard the shuffle of clothes as they fell to the floor.

Henry pulled the cup of my bra down and folded it under my breasts, making them stand from my chest. Then he was over me, sitting astride over my hips. I felt his warm flesh against mine and let out my breath. I wanted to feel him inside me. Instead, his fingers gripped my nipples and pinched, pulling them. I stifled a cry. My walls were thin.

"Do you remember your safe word?" His voice was calm and even. Under that even tone, though, I could hear the darkness that swirled in his eyes. It was taunting me, begging me not to use it.

"I remember." I marveled at the internal struggle of the man over me. To be driven by something so deep and powerful inside, to accept the control I handed over, and to still be willing to heed a simple word. Nothing stopped him from ignoring it except for – for what.

He needs me to trust him.

He pinched harder at my nipples and I clenched my teeth. It hurt as he pulled them, but the pain signals turned warm, moving into my shoulder blades, to my spine, and up to my head. There the pain became a pool into which my consciousness dove. He twisted and I grunted, pressing up against him, inviting him to enter me.

"So hungry." He laced his words with delicious venom. As they bit into me, I felt them mingle with the pain.

"Please." Between my legs, I was on fire. I wanted to feel him thrust into me, hard and fast, with no regard for anything except to fill me and take me.

"So polite. I have to be gentle." He taunted me. I grunted as he moved off me. I heard the rip of foil and he was down again, pressing against me.

"Please." I remembered his words; I needed to say what I wanted. "I want it rough."

He eased into me slowly. He felt wonderful there, and I wanted to feel more of him. "Rough? But you are so sweet and polite."

I moaned and he laughed. He was torturing me, and he loved it. I realized that through my frustration, I loved it too. He pulled out slowly and back in again, the motion so wonderful, even as it taunted me.

"Are you mine?" he asked.

The question tossed my mind into the pool that the pain, still throbbing in my nipples, had formed. There I was surrounded by him. I wanted to drown there. He took hold of one nipple and squeezed, demanding an answer from me. It created waves over my body and I clenched around him, feeling an orgasm overtaking me, as slow and steady as his pace. It eased through my body, stirring the pool in my head.

He pinched harder and twisted. I let out a weak cry as the last of the orgasm shook through my body. From the pool in my mind, I saw everything laid out, Henry, the lawsuit, my fears, and his insecurities. I saw Ana at her desk, managing complaints and damage control with the media. I saw his contacts, shadows, keeping rabid photographers at bay with misdirection and coercion. I saw him and me, standing in the pool of my pain, brought by him, carried by me. Here both of us were exposed, and I felt safe and complete.

"Yes." I was relieved when he did not ease his grip on my nipple. He pulled out and thrust in, hard and fast. I gasped and felt the surge of pleasure move up through my body, stirring all the images in my head back into a jumble. He pulled out and thrust, repeatedly and harder each time. Each impact of his body against mine, hard and painful, was completion.

I gave over to the sensation and to him. There was no point in denying myself or what I wanted. Damage control would manage with me there as much as without.

THREE

I was surprised on Monday morning when I could walk normally. As Henry massaged my inner thighs and pelvis after, he had said it was to manage the effects of the rough sex. I was bruised, and sitting down hurt. Like the stripes from his flogger, however, it left me feeling warm. They were marks, asked for and given. As I walked into the office, I could not help but smile, and the others noticed right away.

"Someone had a good weekend," Karla remarked as I walked over to the planning table.

"It's about time." Lillian gave me a smile.

I said nothing about my night; I just let them state their guesses and theories around me. Nora silenced everyone with a cough. As she was about to start the session, the office door opened. A courier stepped in with a dozen red roses in hand.

"Ms. Caldwell?" He looked nervous under Nora's annoyed gaze.

The appearance of the flowers stunned me. I raised my hand and he brought them over with a quick apology for the interruption. I took them with thanks, and the courier quickly vacated. I took in the scent of the flowers and looked at my team and Nora.

"We won't get anything done until you say who they're from," Nora said.

I smiled. She was not as annoyed as she played, and I saw the curiosity in her eyes as well. I opened the envelope and pulled out the card with the embossed L. On the other side was a simple message that sent a thrill down my spine and between my legs.

For Mine,

Henry

I did not need to say anything for the girls to know who sent the roses. The L on the card was unmistakable. Around me, squeals of delight sounded, and I saw a hint of satisfaction in Nora's eyes as well. Everyone, it seemed, was invested in the success of my strange romance. I wondered if they had an idea of how dark it was, if they would be so excited. Then I remembered that each of them had been with Henry at some point. They knew his proclivities.

I took the roses to my desk and set them neatly. The card I turned so that I would see the message when I worked. As I walked back, I was bombarded by questions. I held up my hands and smiled. My mind was swimming, but I wanted to get to work on the project as much as I knew Nora wanted.

"Yes, we're back together."

Squeals erupted again. Karla promised that we would all celebrate over lunch. Nora reminded us that would only come after the noon deadline she set for us. Everyone quieted and we focused on the task, a proposal to put together and a very demanding client.

I was surprised by my focus through the morning, and everyone seemed to fall in line with the quick pace that I set. The first part of our proposal was complete before noon. Our first hurdle for this project was behind us. At lunch, I shared an abridged version of my Sunday, sans mention of Michael or Henry following me home. I did not go into too much detail. They might all be familiar with Henry's appetites, but I was not comfortable discussing such intimate details.

When we arrived back at the office, a second set of roses sat on my desk, these a bright yellow. The girls oohed as we each walked to our desks. They thought the flowers came from Henry, but I was not so sure. I opened the envelope and pulled out the card.

M

I put the card back into the envelope and contemplated the flowers on my desk. This, I thought, could get very messy.

At the end of the day, I walked down to Henry's office. He had sent me an email shortly before five o'clock. Both sets of flowers were still on my desk, though Henry's card was in my purse. I wanted to keep his message on me. His secretary, Hillary, her soft blonde hair neatly pulled back, gestured for me to enter. I walked into his office as he was hanging up the phone. He stood and walked around his desk as I came in.

"Everyone in the office is buzzing about the flowers you received today," he said.

Heat rushed to my cheeks. "Your card is kind of obvious."

He walked up to me and smiled. He brought his hand behind my head and removed the clip holding my bun in place, letting my hair fall down. I sighed at the sensation of my hair touching my neck and took the clip that he offered me. "So, who was the second set from?"

I coughed as I put the clip into my purse, surprised by the question. I looked up at him. "Michael."

Henry tilted his head to one side and smiled. "Two suitors."

He placed his hand behind my back and guided me to the door. I saw no jealousy in his eyes and marveled. I knew better than to question whether he cared. It made me wonder, then, why he was not concerned. Was it trust, or was it simply that he did not see Michael as a threat?

We left the building separately. I remembered Ana's exclamation, at how easy it was to divert questions about me when reporters did not see me with Henry. I was not eager to add to her workload, and the reporters were not showing any signs of thinning their ranks in the lobby, not yet. I walked up to my car and started down the parking deck. Henry pulled out behind me and we drove to his condominium.

I hated the idea of hiding, and I hoped that it would not bother him. I was happy to be with him again, but I did not relish the idea of reporters in my face. At the opera, they had been polite enough to stay back so that we could walk. I remembered the way they had engulfed Ana and did not expect to fare any better.

When I arrived at his condo, I was relieved to see that he was right. The reporters had abandoned it completely. I pulled into the parking deck and was surprised when the attendant gave me a guest pass without question. I wondered if he recognized me, or if Henry had called ahead on the drive. The latter seemed more likely, and I felt warmed by the forethought. Life had so many little intricacies, and Henry noted each one and accounted for them. Such meticulousness had to be exhausting.

I found a place to park and waited for him inside the lobby of the building. He led me up with the promise of a fresh and warm meal waiting for us upstairs. When he opened the door, the smell of rosemary and roast beef greeted me. I followed him to the dining room table, where two places were set, and a meal of beef, diced potatoes, and fresh vegetables waited for us. It was surprisingly warm and homey compared to the cool opulence around me.

As I sat down, I thought the meal was perfect.

Henry closed the blinds of the windows and brought out sparkling water for us to drink. I waited for him to sit down and we began to serve ourselves from the offering left for us.

"I want to ask you about something," Henry said as he placed slices of the roast onto his plate. "I was not sure about it, but this afternoon told me that I could."

I looked at him curiously. What about this afternoon would have told him anything?

"It was your honesty about the flowers and your discretion about leaving," Henry said, seeming to sense my confusion. "Both of those things are very important to what I want to ask you."

A shiver moved down my body and I sipped my water to try to ground myself. I knew what was coming, and the idea was exciting and terrifying. It was one thing for him to tie me up. That was limited control, one thing for a short time.

"I want to train you to be my submissive," Henry said.

I studied him carefully, measuring his expression. Once again, he was holding down and suppressing the darkness in his eyes. Whatever internal struggle he fought, he was battling it now to control himself. I wondered at that, at why he would only show it at certain times, when I welcomed it so eagerly.

"That's a big word," I said. "What would be involved?"

I took a bite of my food and waited for him to answer. The beef melted in my mouth and I fought the urge to give up the conversation and simply indulge.

"I want to explore that with you. I want to start small, and add to it, as you feel comfortable giving me power. This is all new for you. I could give you a list of things, but it would be meaningless. Even if you know them, you won't have a basis of comparison to know if it is something you can or want to explore. If I introduce them over time, then you can decide based on what you've experienced and how much you trust me."

I swallowed my bite of food. "What if you bring up something that I just don't want to try? I want to talk about things before we add them in."

Henry nodded his head. "Communication is key in this. So is consent. If it is something that you look at and know it is just not something you can do, tell me and we won't do it. If it is something that just scares you, though, I want to try."

I saw the darkness try to rise up in his eyes. This was my chance to learn something new. "Why?"

Henry pulled the darkness down again, and I was afraid he would not tell me. "Fear is the power that other things have over you. I would like it if you gave that power to me."

Another shiver moved through my body. I took a bite of the rosemary potatoes and chewed them. Dominance and submission was power exchange, on a deeper level than just being tied up and smacked with paddles and floggers. I was also understanding that it was more than just giving commands. He wanted power over my fears as well. Would he use them or help me overcome them? I could see Henry delighting from either one. I could see myself giving over to both as well.

"I can do that." I knew my voice did not sound confident, but Henry nodded all the same. This was new to me, but not to him. I supposed that he knew how hard it could be to be subjected to a fear.

"I want to start simple, rituals for when we are together, and the commands that I want you to obey. I want to explore more pain with you. You're my submissive, but you still have your own power. If something is too much, you have your safe word. If you need to step back, if things become too intense, use it."

I finished my meal in silence, contemplating what he said. He did not push me to talk. He simply ate his meal and waited. He did not look uncomfortable with the silence, and the patience that I saw in his eyes was reassuring. I could do this, I realized. In a way, it was the game we were already playing, but in small measure. Now, we were going to be moving it to another level.

When we finished our meal, he brought me to the middle of the enormous room that dominated his condo. He told me to strip and I removed my clothes, folding them neatly for him to take away. I remembered that I still had a change of clothes here, from the last time I had spent the night. I wondered if I would be staying tonight as well.

I stood naked, exposed to him. Henry walked around me and I could not help but look down. I felt strange standing here, and his manner seemed so odd, powerful, appraising, and cold.

"Is it comfortable to look down?" His voice had an inquiring tone.

"Yes."

"Then look up. I want your head even, your eyes forward. You may not raise them to look in my eyes, but if I engage your eyes, you will not look away." I raised my head up and looked straight ahead, my eyes focused on the kitchen. To make his point, Henry stopped his pacing and fixed his eyes on me. I did not look up to his eyes until he brought his head down to meet mine. He straightened again and I followed him with my eyes, careful not to break contact.

"Very good. Understanding when to make eye contact and when to look away is important. Averting your eyes can be a sign of respect or a signal for deception. I want you always open and honest with me. I will signal you when I want eye contact by meeting your line of sight. You will always keep your head even in my presence so that I do not have to be below you to look into your eyes. You should always be willing to let your Dominant come down to your level, but you should never make Him lower Himself beneath you."

I nodded, keeping my eyes on his.

"You may look away," he said. When I did, he continued. "When I bring you here, you are to immediately remove your clothing. I want you naked before me. At any time, I want to enjoy your body. You will stay naked until you leave or we go out somewhere. Sometimes people will come into the condo. Servants will be here shortly to clear our dinner away. I sometimes have guests come up. They are always close friends, people that I trust. I never bring strangers or mere business associates here. You will not hide your nakedness from the servants or the guests." I darted my eyes up to him with a gasp. His eyes narrowed and I turned them back quickly to look ahead. "Servants are beneath your notice as my submissive. Their role is to simply do their work and leave, heedless of what takes place around them. My guests are to see what is mine. I won't lie. I like to boast. I will not be sharing you with them and they will not be allowed to touch you."

The thought of others seeing me naked in his apartment made me shiver. I clenched my fists and tried to control it. I focused on the idea. Was I just scared, or was it something I simply could not do? I decided it was fear. That, I could give to him. I nodded, keeping my eyes focused forward.

"This is how we will begin, then," Henry said. "I will delight in your body and use it. We will explore sensations of pleasure and pain. You will submit to me by being open."

He walked to the kitchen counter and picked up the small black remote that controlled the blinds. He pressed a button and I watched as they opened and lifted. I closed my eyes and clenched my fists tightly. Tears rolled down my cheeks as my nakedness was exposed to the city. It was foolish, I knew. We were several stories above the closest building; no one could see us. That still did not change the way that it felt.

Henry walked up to me and placed a finger on my cheek, lifting away a tear. I opened my eyes to see him at eye level. I followed him as he straightened up again. His eyes swirled, and I understood that this was a fear he was enjoying. As I kept my eyes focused on his, I began to feel warm, and safe. I was not merely a naked woman before an open window. I was His naked woman before His open window.

"To your knees." His voice was steady. I lowered myself to my knees, still keeping my eyes on his and tucking my heels under my buttocks to support myself. "Very good. Place your hands behind your back. Keep the palms out, but overlap the wrists."

I did as he told me. He unfastened his pants and bid me to look down. I watched as he pushed his pants open and pulled out his cock, hard and erect. My breathing quickened. I knew what he wanted, but I held myself back, waiting for his command. He did not use words this time. He brought himself closer and pressed into my lips. I opened my mouth and welcomed him, sucking him, and rolling my tongue around to taste him. He was rich and I savored him as he gently pushed deeper, forcing me to widen my throat to take him. When he came, I sucked harder, feeling him issue onto my tongue and the back of my throat. When he did not pull out after, I continued, relishing the taste of him and bringing him back to his hardness and pleasure once more.

When he finished, he pulled out of my mouth. I licked my lips, looking at him still wet. Henry guided me to stand up, and I did, lifting by one knee and then the other, keeping my hands behind me. Henry led me to the bedroom and I followed, wondering what he would do next. He led me to stand under the eyehook and I watched as he opened his black trunk and looked through his tools.

He took out the black rope and brought it over. Behind my back, he tied my hands together at the wrist, forming a wide cuff around them. He tightened it and brought the rope up through the eyehook. I watched as he tied it off to the iron footboard, pulling so that my arms pulled up behind my back and forced me to lean forward.

"Very beautiful," Henry said. He brought his hand between my legs and pushed them apart until I was standing flat on the balls of my feet. "Can you breathe okay?"

"Yes." I was surprised at the complexity of this binding. I balanced on my feet and pulled with my arms to hold myself up. It was tiring, but the strain was all in my arms and legs. With time, I would spread, but I doubted I would be restrained long enough for that to happen.

Henry turned to his chest and brought out a new toy. I recognized a riding crop immediately and felt afraid. He brought it around and struck gently along my left buttock, using only the tip. I sighed and he struck hard, the resounding pop of the cracker accentuating the quick, sharp pain. It was not as severe as the flogger was. He struck again in the same location, and again. Each impact added to the one before. I cried out as the sharp pain began to intensify, and shudder as it began to warm through my body. He moved to the other buttock, striking soft first, and then hard, repeatedly over the same spot. I cried out again as the pain grew and spread warm over my body. It was bliss striking my skin.

He struck between my legs, the impact moving over my labia and teasing my clitoris. My eyes flew open wide and I gasped loudly. He struck again and I moaned. The pain and the pressure of impact combined. I wanted to feel him drive inside me and he struck again, a little harder this time. My knees wanted to buckle and I struggled to keep them straight. My arms could not take all of my weight. He struck me again and I groaned, wanting more.

"Harder please." I uttered the words before I realized what I was saying.

"As you wish." His voice was even, deep, and cruel. I imagined the darkness filling his eyes and he struck between my legs, harder than before. I screamed and my body shuddered. He struck me again, and again. The pain and the pleasure filled my head until I was drowning in them. Another strike, and another and I felt the tremors of my orgasm overtake me. One more strike pushed it through, a red wave of pleasure and pain that drew out a loud, long scream from my lips.

Then he was easing me back. The rope was untied, and I realized that I had blacked out, on my feet. Henry held onto my waist as he threaded the rope back through the eyehook and loosened the cuffs around my wrists. The rope fell onto the floor and he picked me up, carrying me to the bed and laying me down gently.

My head still swam. I tried to say something but could not get the words out. I watched him as he moved to his nightstand and pulled out a tube of something clear. He dabbed it on his fingers and brought it between my legs. It felt cool and soothing, and the throbbing there slowly eased into a light and steady pulse.

He kissed my lips and I felt the tide in my head recede. He met my eyes and once again I saw the darkness receded, sated and chased away. Gently he eased the blankets beneath my body and brought them over me. I tried to speak again, to ask him to lay down. He undressed and climbed under the covers next to me. He picked up a remote and clicked it, lowering the lights around us. Then he brought me close to him, draping my body over him, and cooing softly in my ear, bringing me back into my mind.

I wanted him inside me, but as he brushed my hair slowly, I felt exhaustion overtake me. I listened to him breath and closed my eyes, the waves of sleep slowly carrying me away.

FOUR

My week was divided between work and Henry. Wednesday and Thursday night, he wanted me at his condo, to continue my training. By Thursday, I was comfortable standing naked in front of his window. No servants had yet appeared while I was naked. On Monday, they had not come in until he had taken me to the bedroom. I knew it would only be a matter of time before it happened, or he had a guest over. He was easing me into it, allowing me time to be comfortable, and for that, I was thankful.

I was enjoying this role so far. On Thursday, I felt giddy as I stripped for him, ready to stand and allow him to inspect me. He walked around me, quietly observing my body, just as he had the night before. I wanted him to touch me, but I knew this was not the time to ask. That would come later, when we discussed the evening. He was experienced; all of this was new for me. I quickly understood that this was a learning experience for him as well. He knew what it was to be Dominant, but he had to learn what it was to be my Dominant as much as I had to learn to be his submissive.

I did not see him for the weekend, even though he was in town. There were still parts of his life that were kept apart from me. Even though he was bringing me into this deep and intimate role, there were things that I was not privy to. I knew some of it was the lawsuit, and I wished that he would open up to me about it. Other times, it was whatever he did socially, and I had no idea what that was. I was beginning to develop strong feelings for him. I dared to tell myself that I was falling in love, and my submission to him was only heightening it.

I enjoyed time with my friends on Saturday. I noticed that our group was thinning. Typically anywhere from seven to fourteen of us would get together to wander the clubs downtown. Two were gone for good, it seemed. One was moving out of state, the other had picked up a job that required evenings and weekends. As nine of us managed Saturday night together, I wondered who would be next to leave our little group.

On Sunday, Michael invited me to lunch. I accepted. I saw no reason not to. The flowers did not bother Henry, and if I were around Michael, I could keep things strictly calm. As we enjoyed our lunch, I wondered if that were going to be so easy. He was not shy about his intentions, even when I gently put him down. I liked where things were going with Henry, and I did not want to change it or give it up. At the same time, I saw something with Michael that Henry was not offering. Michael was willing to share. He talked eagerly about his life and about himself.

It was night and day between him and Henry. I could see how Michael and I could work. He was sincere and simple in his tastes. There were no complex rituals, no rules of obedience and punishment. No safe words, no wondering if neighbors might hear. The simplicity was in its own way as tempting as the darkness that stirred Henry.

By Monday, the confusion that stirred my emotions was calmed. I focused on work and was happy to see the message from Henry that he wanted to see me that night. I would be spending the night with him again, which meant more training. I decided that I would tell him about my lunch with Michael, and what each of our intentions was. He had told me that my honesty was part of what made him decide that I could be his submissive. I did not want to shatter that.

The reporters were thinned out by the time I left the building, and I was surprised by that. The crowd this morning had been just as thick and energetic as the crowd last week. I doubted, however, that it was a sign of lessened media interest. Most likely, they were looking for other avenues to get their scoops and stories.

I drove to Henry's condominium and found him ready to greet me. When I arrived, I stripped obediently and waited for him to inspect me. This time he touched me, lifting my breasts, and examining my nipples. He reached between my legs and parted the lips of my labia gently, and then parting my buttocks to examine me there as well. The whole exercise was erotic and it left me flustered and aroused. When he was finished, he guided me to the table where sushi waited for us.

"I saw Michael yesterday," I said, as the small talk that started our dinner dissipated. He looked up at me and cocked an eyebrow. "It was just lunch, but I thought after the flowers I should tell you."

Henry nodded his head and swallowed his bite of sushi. "I appreciate that. He's doing well, I take it?"

"He's enjoying his position at Lellman& White," I said. I picked up another bite of sushi with my chopsticks.

"Interesting choice in employers." Michael's eyes stirred and I thought I saw a hint of something there.

It did not look like jealousy, though it was close. Protectiveness? I thought so. I hoped that his caution was more about the current ownership of Lellman& White, and not about Lellman& White being the company where I interned. To me, the former was of greater concern. Ternion Communications had much more reason to look at Michael for his past employment than Michael had to look at Lellman& White for me.

"He's not talking to the media about you, though," Henry said. "That at least shows that his intentions are honorable."

I smiled. "You don't mind me having lunch or something like that from time to time?"

Henry placed his hands on the table and looked at me evenly. Once more, the darkness in his eyes looked suppressed to me. "Stacy, you are my submissive, and that requires us both to be committed to that relationship. I will ask if you want to give me more control as we go along. You may even ask me if you can give over more control. One thing I will not do is tell you who you can socialize with or who you can be friends with. That is your decision."

I felt warm from his answer. A simple "no" would have sufficed, but this was so much better. This told me so many things, about how serious he was about this relationship, and a little more of what he expected of me.

"How would you like to go to a party with me this weekend?" Henry's tone changed as the conversation changed. My ears perked up at the question. This was finally a chance to see into the rest of Henry Lennox's world.

"I would like that."

"This is my kind of party," Henry's voice took on an air of caution, "that is, everyone who is attending the party is involved in the lifestyle in some way. Most people will be Dominants and their submissives or slaves. We have a few people who are professional fetishists, models, exhibitionist, that sort of thing."

The idea sounded intriguing. I tried to imagine what this type of party would be like. "What do I do there?"

"Mostly, you stay by my side. You will be expected to keep your eyes averted downward. Only address a Dominant if they address you first, and they should not do so without addressing me. You can speak to other submissives freely, of course. Protocol at parties like this is strict, and you will be able to tell quickly who is what. You can address me freely. You can just call me Henry; you don't have to address me as any specific title. I want that to come naturally from you."

I nodded, understanding, and swallowed another bite of sushi. "Will I be wearing a collar?"

The idea of a collar was exciting to me. I had been studying more about Dominance and submission and reading books at home. Collars were not uncommon at parties and denoted who was owned and who was not.

"No. I'm not ready to give you a collar yet. That is another level of commitment." My expression dropped. I wondered why I was not worthy yet to have a collar. He claimed me as his already. He loved to refer to me that way, and I loved hearing the words. He touched my hand gently as he spoke again. "Giving and receiving a collar is like a marriage. I don't do training collars either. I have only ever collared one woman, and I want to be sure that when I collar another, she does not decide later to give it back."

I met Henry's eyes and felt my confidence return. It was me, but it was him as well. It was not a matter of worth. It was whether or not we would both stay committed to this relationship. We continued eating, Henry telling me more about the party, and what to expect. I listened as best as I could and hoped that I would be able to remember everything for him.

I pulled at the hem of my skirt and fidgeted in my heels. I was nervous. I was excited while Henry was dressing me. I felt sexy, wearing a skirt that came down mid-thigh and flared out. I wore a black lace halter over it, and sheer thigh highs underneath. I was not allowed to wear panties, and Henry warned me that at any time during the party, he might touch me. I was not to act startled or ashamed when he did, and that I needed to tell him then if I was not comfortable with the idea. As I stared at myself in the mirror, I thought the idea was wonderful.

Now I was beginning to doubt my convictions.

"You will be fine," Henry said as the elevator doors closed. He turned me around and tilted my face up to him. "You need to stop pulling at your skirt. Keep your shoulders straight, your head tilted down slightly, and relax. I'm not going to embarrass you, and I know you will not embarrass me."

I breathed in and out slowly to relax. The elevator doors opened and I waited for Henry to step off the elevator. I stepped off behind him. I would be expected to stand just behind and to his left, and so I wanted to practice that now. The side, he told me, was a preference. He preferred to turn to his left to see me, and being right handed, he wanted that hand closest to him, as a sign of my readiness to serve him.

I followed him down the hall and to the suite that waited for us. The hotel was incredible, and I expected the suite would be breathtaking. He knocked on the door and Ana answered. I was startled to see her. She smiled at Henry, keeping her head high. She was a Dominant, then. I wondered if that explained the type of discipline I sensed in the office. Was she responsible for those hints that I picked up? I kept my head tilted slightly and my eyes averted.

"Stacy, it's wonderful to see you." Her voice sounded sincere, and I smiled. It made me glad to know that she was not displeased that Henry and I were together again.

Henry coughed. I peeked up under my eyelashes to see Ana give him a sheepish look.

"Please forgive me," Ana said to him.

Henry gave her a warm smile. "*You* can address Stacy any time you like."

Ana gave Henry a smirk and turned her attention back to me. I quickly averted my eyes again. "Welcome."

She stepped aside and we entered the room. I raised my head a little so that I could look around. I saw several men and women, a few alone but most in pairs. Some women held their heads high, others slightly downturned. From them, I noticed that I only needed to tilt mine slightly, and adjusted my posture accordingly. Some men kept the same posture as well, and I marveled. Intellectually, I knew male submissives existed, but I could not imagine how it worked. Most men I knew were aggressive and boisterous. These were as quiet as the women were.

I followed Henry as he walked around the room, mingling with other guests. He was relaxed here, and I marveled at the change in his demeanor. The protocol and formality that had me so nervous was second nature to him. As he spoke to people, he introduced me as his submissive. I felt goose bumps each time he spoke the word. No one asked about a collar and no one mentioned the lawsuit or the media frenzy. Everyone was courteous and respectful of Henry and of me.

After a while, a few of the submissives pulled me away from him gently. I was nervous, ready for a thousand questions about Henry. Instead, they were curious about me. I relaxed and talked. As they shared their experiences, I listened. One offered tips on how she remembered party protocols. Another discussed sub-space with me, something that I realized I had experienced often with Henry, even though I did not have a name for it at the time.

A couple of hours into the party, I was relaxed. I could have been clubbing with my friends from college, though in a way, this felt more natural. Even with the rules and the expectations, I felt more myself here than anywhere else, except perhaps in the office. When I asked one of the submissives a question about thoughts or an emotion I experienced, she understood right away.

"I call it the dragon," Cheryl said. She was a cute strawberry blonde with luscious curves and an infectious smile. "When I see it in my Sir's eyes, I get weak in the knees. I look for ways to draw it out because it's dangerous."

I felt so relieved that I was not alone in noticing that something deep, that something worthy of being feared, and wanting to touch it. I was strange, but I was starting to understand that we were all strange in this room. We were strange for the kinks and fetishes that we enjoyed. We were strange for the way that we saw this lifestyle as a dark reflection of the rest of the world. We were strange, different, and unique. We were not alone, and that was a relief to me.

Henry came around to me and politely excused me from the company of the other submissives. I followed, asking how he was enjoying the party.

"I felt bad that I was not with you," he said. "You look like you were enjoying yourself, though, so that's good."

Now I felt like I had abandoned him. "I'm sorry. I should have come back over."

Henry stopped and looked down at me. I glanced up, feeling that I was supposed to meet his eyes and he smiled. "I'm here; I'm fine. It's you that I wanted to make sure enjoyed herself."

He started walking again and I followed. He walked up to a tall woman with long, straight, deep brown hair and piercing ice-blue eyes. She was a little taller than Henry and strikingly beautiful. As we approached her, I was sure to avert my eyes. She had a fierce bearing, and I realized that I did not want to see her displeasure.

"Mistress Aevia," Henry offered her a slight bow, "I would like to present my submissive, Stacy."

I stood still, my head tilted slightly, my hands open and behind my back. I felt her eyes burn into me and understood one thing very quickly, even without having to look up to her. She tapped her finger against her hip in a quick, rhythmic motion.

"Isn't she precious?" I could hear the venom in Mistress Aevia's voice and I did not want to chase it. She did not approve of me. I looked down to see Henry's fist tighten. She must have seen something in his face. When she spoke again, her voice softened, for him at least. "Still, you have always had the penchant for picking up strays and nurturing them. I hope that she's worth all of the trouble she has been."

"She already is." Henry's words were a comfort, but I did not miss the hint of deference in his voice. He respected Mistress Aevia, which meant that her opinion would matter to him. I felt my heart sink and wanted to be anywhere else.

"So you say. Ah, there is dear Ana." Mistress Aevia stepped aside. "Enjoy your pet."

She walked away and I felt relieved. Henry walked to the balcony and I followed him outside and onto the quiet porch. He leaned against the railing, looking out over the city. I took my place next to him, letting my gaze follow his.

"Did I do something wrong?" I asked at last.

Henry turned to look at me. I saw him bring his face down and turned to meet his eyes. "You did nothing wrong, but I should have defended you better."

I thought about the exchange. I was new to this lifestyle, but I was not new to women like Mistress Aevia. They existed everywhere. They had an inflated sense of their own importance. It did not matter if it was deserved or not. They believed that it gave them the right to pass judgment on anyone, and woe if anyone challenged them. No, what he had said was fine. Anything more would have caused a scene, one that she would likely spin to prove her point.

"You defended me perfectly," I said.

"I hoped she would be nicer to you. Mistress Aevia is the one who trained me when I first found the lifestyle. She's a professional fetishist, respected here and in many other cities. I should have remembered that she is also exacting and hard to please." Henry took my hands in his and kissed the back of them.

I remembered that he told me once that he had only been obsessed with one other woman. It was obvious to me that Mistress Aevia had been that one. I felt something strange stir in my gut. As I thought that she did not deserve his obsession, I realized what it was. I had almost forgotten what it felt like, even though for much of my young life it plagued me like an ill begotten friend.

Jealousy.

I followed Henry back inside and we rejoined the party. While the protocol of the evening was still in place, the atmosphere seemed more relaxed. I did not know if it was because Mistress Aevia had apparently found another part of the suite to entertain herself in, or because some of the guests were giving small demonstrations within their groups. One Dominant had her submissive down on his hands and knees. Her legs rested comfortably across his back. Another had a paddle and was using it to show a young couple proper striking areas on the bare and exposed backside of his submissive.

Henry sat down in a chair and bid me to stand to his right. Another man joined him. I did not miss the look that he gave me as he sat down, and was happy to avert my eyes. The lust there was clear. He looked familiar, and my mind struggled to place the face. I chanced a glance down at Henry as the two began to speak, talking like old friends, and saw darkness stirring in his eyes. As they talked about their different business conquests, Henry's hand rose slowly up my leg. I steadied my breathing as it moved up between them and found its place, warm, wet, and eagerly waiting for him.

This, I understood, was Henry's demonstration, his ownership of my body. As his fingers slipped easily into me, emotions flooded me. My heartbeat raced. I kept calm and focused on his voice as he spoke, even and confident. He pushed his finger forward, and I could feel my knees want to buckle. His touch was delicious and I wanted to give over to it. I also knew that was something I could not do. I counted in my head, focused on the tone of his words, anything to keep the swelling pleasure at his fingers from over taking me.

Then I felt it, warmth moving over my body slow and smooth. I flexed my fingers and clenched my teeth to keep from moaning or crying out. He slipped his finger out of me and up toward my clit. Every part of me seemed alive from the orgasm he had brought on, and I struggled to keep myself still and calm. He stopped before he reached my clitoris and pulled his finger back down, his touch fire and ice on my skin, before slipping his finger back inside me. I felt a tremble begin and took a slow, deep breath.

Their conversation ended. The other man started to stand and paused. "May I address your submissive?"

"Of course." Henry kept his fingers inside of me. I felt terrified. I knew that I would be expect to answer or to say something. I had no idea if my voice would work.

"Miss Stacy, it is a pleasure to meet you." The man gave a slight bow, and when he did, he met my eyes for only a moment. When he rose again, I did not raise my eyes with him. I was not sure if it would be appropriate. Henry pushed his fingers deeper into me and I fought to keep myself steady. "You are a credit to Henry, and I hope that he appreciates you."

With that, he turned and walked away, not waiting for me to reply to him. Slowly, Henry removed his fingers, sliding them through the inner layers of my skirt. He stood, and with his right hand took mine.

"Are you ready to go?" he asked me gently. I could hear want in his voice.

"Yes." My heart pounded in my chest at his display. I knew that I should be embarrassed by it, indignant at the casual way he played with my body. I also knew that it was exciting. Some part of me wanted to do it again. I thought of his promise that he would have guests while I was with him. I wondered what things he would have me do as he spoke to them.

Henry led me out, giving a few goodbyes as we walked past people. He was silent as we walked to the elevator, and I wondered if everything was okay. He pressed the button and when the elevator door opened, I followed him inside.

When the door closed, my world was full of him. He brought his arms around me, gripping my hair and holding me in place as he kissed me, pressing his body against me and pushing me into the wall of the elevator. I welcomed his tongue and the passion with which his body tried to absorb mine. I wanted to unfasten his pants, to push them down and have him take me here, and hesitated. I thought of all the shots of elevator footage. The last thing he needed was the hotel selling a sex video to one of the tabloids.

He released me when the elevator dinged for the lobby. I straightened my hair as the doors opened and pushed down my skirt. He walked out quietly and I followed him. I was eager for more of him. He felt wild in the elevator, alive in a way that I had not experienced before. We walked quietly to the car and he opened the passenger door for me. I climbed in and sat down. He closed it and walked around to his own.

When he sat down and closed the door, I started to move toward him. I wanted him now. I needed to feel that fire again. He placed his hand on my arm and eased me back down into my seat. "Not here." He turned to me. His eyes swirled, the green of his eyes so dark that I could barely make that out as the color now. "What I want to do to you, I can't do here."

My heart leapt into my throat and I could not push out words. I sat back in my chair and fastened my seatbelt. Henry pulled out of the parking lot and started the drive home. When we were out of the deck and onto the road, he moved his hand and placed it between my legs, holding it there, touching, but not playing.

The drive uptown seemed to take forever tonight. When we finally pulled into the parking deck of his building, I felt as though I had been in the car forever, drowning in my frustration and desire. I followed Henry out and up to his condominium on the top floor of the building. When he opened the door and I walked inside, I did not wait. I began removing my clothing, careful for the delicate material of the halter and the skirt. Henry took them from me as I removed them and walked through the door from the kitchen. I walked to the center of the room and waited for my inspection.

Henry walked up to me and invited my eyes up to him. "You've already had your inspection this evening." His eyes were still deep and dark. I was so afraid of him pushing it down. "You were lovely at the party, so much more that I could have asked. What you let me do to you was daring and naughty, and I have a punishment that I want to use for it."

Now I understood his desire to wait. I nodded.

"It is called Bastinado. It is very painful. I can use many different implements, but I prefer a narrow paddle that I own. It is light, swift, and sharp. I will use it to strike the soles of your feet, between your arches, while I have your feet bound."

I said nothing. I thought of what he described. He did not warn me about pain often. It was usually to be assumed. I imagined, then, that it had to be severe. He took my hand and I stepped forward to follow him to the bedroom. He laid me down on the bed and went to his trunk of tools. He pulled out cuffs, a narrow bar with more cuffs on both ends, and a thin, narrow black paddle lined with leather.

He brought the loose cuffs to my wrists and bound them securely. He then pulled my arms straight up and clipped the cuffs together by their short chains behind one of the posts of his iron bed. He brought the bar to my feet and slipped the cuffs around my ankles, tightening them carefully. The bar kept my legs apart. He had told me about this device, and the many ways it could be used, but this was the first time he had decided to use it.

Henry raised my legs by the bar and picked up the thin paddle. He tapped it lightly against the arch of my left foot several times, and I sighed. The sensation was firm and pleasant. Then he brought the paddle back a few inches and struck, hard and sharp. The pain surged through my foot and up my leg. He followed it by another strike and I screamed. This was intense, unlike any other strike I had felt. There was no pleasurable warmth to follow the strike, only the pain, sharp and harsh. He struck me three more times and I opened my mouth to utter my safe word.

Before I could, he shifted, moving to my other foot. I closed my mouth and felt the sharp pain begin to spread and dull. Now, the warmth came, easing into my arch like an old friend. He tapped my right food lightly, several times again and I understood the purpose. It was to warm up my foot, to excite the nerve endings and relax the muscles. When he struck, I screamed again. The pain was intense. I imagined that he was pulling back to his shoulder, but when I opened my eyes, I saw again he was only pulling back a few inches.

He struck again, and I saw that the darkness had overtaken his eyes. I cried out as the struck three more times. Again, I opened my mouth to speak, but he was already lowering the paddle. He dropped it onto the bed and took my feet into his hands, rubbing over the point of impact gently, easing the warmth into the rest of my foot. I looked up into his eyes to see the darkness easing.

Henry gently set my feet down. They felt sore and warm from his strikes and the gentle rub that followed. I watched him remove his clothing and open the small foil packet. I hated that thing. I wanted to feel him, bare inside me. I thought of how he felt on my tongue and closed my eyes. The condom was just another barrier, like the silence he kept about himself.

However, those barriers were breaking. Tonight he had brought me into his world. He shared it with me and this, I understood, was his expression of gratitude that I took part in it. He took hold of the spreader bar and raised up my legs, pushing them toward my body, bending my knees, so that I was exposed to him. He entered me fast and hard, and I cried out again for the pleasure of it. He was hard and fast as he pulled out and entered. I gave over to the feeling, letting my cries and shouts ring out, savoring each push into my body. I tightened around him and felt the rush of pleasure, up my body with his thrusts and brushing out, forming goose bumps on my skin. Each thrust pushed more of it through me until I felt him pulse inside me. He held himself inside of me and shook, his body trembling from his effort and pleasure.

Slowly Henry pulled out of me and lay down beside me. He breathed heavily and when I looked over, I saw the darkness settled and the green of his eyes turning bright once again. He turned to look at me and kissed me, softly on the lips. When he pulled away, I licked my lips to still taste him there.

I stretched my legs out and relaxed in my bonds, letting my mind float on the pain and pleasure of my evening. When I turned again to look at him, he stared at the ceiling, his hands folded over his chest. He looked like he was contemplating and I wondered if his mind went through a period of processing, the way that mine did.

"Why didn't you use your safe word?" He turned to look at me. His eyes were clear, serious, and full of concern.

"Why did you stop before I needed to use it?" I kept my eyes focused on his.

He turned and looked back up to the ceiling. I wished that he would not, but I thought he needed to. He was reaching down into himself, understanding me, understanding us. I waited patiently for him to speak. "I didn't need more."

I thought of the pain I endured on my feet. He could have delivered so much more.

"I could do more, but the feeling changes and turns. It's not what I want. Where you carry me, it brings me to that edge. I feel alive and on fire." He turned to look at me again. "I'm afraid that I'm hurting you."

I pulled at my bonds. I wanted to bring my hands down to him and could not. Henry smiled. A little of the darkness stirred and then calmed. His dragon was sated, it seemed. "It hurts, but you don't hurt me. Sometimes I think I could take more. Not tonight. I was about to call out red when you switched feet and stopped. But sometimes."

Henry sat up and began to unfasten my cuffs. He freed my wrists and my ankles. I twisted and turned everything to loosen them. My feet still hurt, but the pain was a light throb now. By morning, it would be gone. Henry stepped out of the room to his bathroom and then back in again, that cursed sheath gone. I still wanted to feel just him, but resigned myself to acceptance. One day, perhaps.

Henry pulled the bedspread down under me and brought it and the sheets over our bodies. He reached out to the bedside table and pushed the button on the remote. Slowly the lights began to dim. He pulled me to him, and I rolled over to snuggle against his body. I closed my eyes and listened to the sound of Henry's breathing as sleep slowly overtook me.

FIVE

On Monday, the party still spun through my mind. It was an amazing place, strange in its formality and display. As my mind processed the weekend, I felt like Alice through the looking glass. It had seemed so perfect there, but I knew that his world could have a dark underside, just like any. I wondered if Mistress Aevia was part of that. I doubted it. If she had trained Henry, she could not be so bad. It was my jealousy, perhaps.

I focused on work and watched my day speed by. There would be no time with Henry tonight. He would be seeing Mistress Aevia. I tried to keep my jealousy down with the thought that I would be spending Wednesday and Thursday both with him. Instead, I would use tonight to do the things that I neglected over the weekend, grocery shopping, and laundry.

After work, I stopped by the market near my apartment. As I picked over tomatoes, I heard a familiar voice behind me.

"Small world."

I turned and smiled to see Michael. I was still too elated from my weekend to let complications bother me. He had a basket with a selection of produce. "Shopping too, I see."

"A few extras on the way home. I happened to see you and thought I would come over." He ran his finger over the bell peppers and picked one out. "Are you doing anything Friday night? I thought I might take you to dinner and a movie."

A date? The complications decided to rear their heads whether I cared about them or not. I offered Michael another smile and shook my head. "That sounds nice, but I really can't."

He frowned deeply. "Henry?"

I nodded and picked out my tomatoes.

"I'd heard rumors," he said. "Is it official then?"

I moved on to avocadoes. I thought of our talk about collars and shrugged my shoulders. "Not really, but I don't like to complicate things."

Michael picked out a tomato. "Do you think he has the same concerns?"

I thought about Mistress Aevia. Would they be playing a game of who could whip harder? Perhaps they took turns giving over to each other, or just enjoyed rough sex. I pushed those though from my mind. Thinking about her was going to do me no good. I had not asked Henry for exclusivity, so I certainly had no right to expect it or be jealous if he took advantage of an evening with an old flame. Besides, Michael was not trying to ask Henry out, he was trying to ask me out. I did not want to complicate my emotional life any more than it was. Henry could run his how he saw fit.

"I'm sorry, that wasn't fair." Michael leaned against the produce counter. "I just worry about you. How long do you think this thing with you and Henry will last? A few weeks, a few months?"

"I don't know." I turned to face Michael. "I'm not asking that question right now. That's not the point anyway. I only want to focus my energy on one person, and that's him."

Michael nodded. "I have to respect that, I suppose." Henry stood back straight. "I have to go, but remember. When he finally breaks your heart, I'm right here."

Michael left before I could say anything else. I did not want to know that he was waiting there in the wings. I did not need him there. I just wanted him to be a friend, and I wondered if he would be satisfied with that.

Slowly, life began to settle into a kind of normalcy. I had my nights with Henry, which were becoming wonderfully sensual explorations. One night, he would have some new sensation, not for pain, but to delight me. He showed me the tool in his trunk that I had taken for a screwdriver. He called it a violet wand, and it reminded me of the static electricity balls I would see in stores at the mall growing up. This ran static electricity up a glass tube. When he touched it to my body, everything came to life. I shivered and moaned as he found different places to touch and test.

Other nights, we would explore pain. Often it would be new modes of impact play. Other times it would be finding new ways to clamp and pinch my skin. He would fold open my labia with clamps, which was excruciating and delicious at once. He showed me his collection of needles, and to that, I had to say no. Not a permanent no, but I was not ready for that yet. He had taken me to another event, this one demonstrating needle and knife play. It looked fascinating, but I saw something between the performers. I could not touch on it, but I sensed a deeper level of intimacy. As deep of a bond as I felt myself forming with Henry, I knew we were not there yet.

There was still so much about him I did not know or understand. As much as we explored sensations, we did not deepen the Dominance and submission side of our relationship. Sometimes I wondered if we would, or if this was the level that it would stay. My attraction for him stretched outside of my submission. If my submission could not deepen, what would that mean for the rest of our relationship?

Henry took me to another party as well, and Mistress Aevia was there. She did not hesitate to hide her displeasure, and Henry bristled under her disapproval of me. I placed my hand in his to keep him calm, to reassure him that it was okay. His was the only approval I needed. I did not have to prove myself to anyone else. Other submissives, who had caught onto her coldness around me, had been sure to remind me of that fact. I did not belong to her; I belonged to him. At the end of the day, he was the only one I had to please.

It all seemed so much to manage, this new world with him. Somehow, I found myself learning. I felt relieved that other submissives were eager to offer advice and tips. I helped me manage my nervousness and navigate this strange place.

I had a routine with work as well. My relationship with Henry had not taken away the focus with which I threw myself into projects, and my team quickly adapted to how I worked, tossing ideas around me when I threw myself into creating a layout, so that I picked them up and implemented them as I could. Karla matched pace with me, and the two of us became the drawing boards for everyone's ideas. It created a unique energy and flow that I enjoyed immensely. Nora was pleased, as even our toughest client had been impressed with our work.

Michael finally seemed to fill a niche in my life as well. He made no other overtures since our conversation at the grocery store. He had said his piece and seemed content to wait and let the chips fall where they may. We were friends. That was enough for me, and he seemed to accept that would be all he would have. We enjoyed coffee on the weekends, usually on Sundays, were we talked about our weeks.

Only my friends from college caused me real worry. We would get together either Friday or Saturday night to wander the clubs. I had begun noticing friends drifting away a few weeks ago, and the trend was still continuing. Their lives were pulling them away as they started careers and chased after people to start families with. We were all growing up, and that meant growing apart as well, it seemed.

SIX

I sat in my apartment, resting from another busy week of work and submissive training and reflected on everything. I was tired, but it was a good tired. We had another project under our belts. Henry and I had found a new level to impact play. I still had a welt on my thigh from his new flogger, and I kept ointment on it as he instructed. The device was a mean one, its tails made of thinner and heavier strips. The welt it left was healing, but I thought I might have a light scar. The idea sent a thrill up and down my spine.

I still did not have the full emotional connection that I wanted with him yet. I had tried to probe, to get him to open up about some aspect of his life, perhaps what had drawn him into the BDSM lifestyle. His eyes would grow dark and he would turn the conversation around again to me or to something else. I knew that I needed that deeper connection with him, but I was unsure how to tell him. I was afraid of seeming clingy or making him think he was inadequate as a Dominant. I did not feel that way at all.

I was beginning to understand why we were in a holding pattern. I was still becoming accustomed to his control. I knew he did not want to move into another level until I was ready. I thought that I might be the one to ask. He had mentioned that I might want to, and it occurred to me that he was waiting to see if I would.

I liked that idea. He told me that control was not taken by the Dominant. It was given by the submissive and then wielded. It would make sense, then, that I would be the one to ask, at least at first. Later, when he understood how I transitioned, he might bring up the subject. The only thing that I was not sure of is what control I wanted to give to him next.

A horn sounded outside of my apartment. I recognized the sound of Lewis' car. I stood up and grabbed my keys. I had my clubbing wallet stuffed into my back pocket with my ID, one credit card, and some emergency cash. I locked the door and stuffed the keys into the pocket of my jeans. I waved to the car and headed down. Trin, who had been my roommate in college, opened the back door and I climbed inside. Six of us total were piled into Lewis' car. When we arrived at the midtown strip, Jake's car, with five more, joined us.

The clubs were busy tonight, more so than usual. I found it curious, but crowds fluctuated sometimes. Most likely, one had some live show to draw out the extra crowds. We made our way into one, ordering drinks and then invading the dance floor, letting our bodies move to the sounds of a techno-mixed pop beat. I could not name the song, and did not even care. I let it carry me as I danced and enjoyed the revelry with my friends.

Trin pulled me to the restrooms after we finished a dance. She primped in front of the mirror and waited for people to clear out of stalls. I knew her well enough to know that this was Trin-speak for "I want to talk to you." The last stall cleared out. When no one else came in, she turned to me.

"Henry Lennox?"

I smiled in spite of myself. Trin's mouth dropped open and she turned from side to side. I laughed at her schoolgirl excitement, but I understood where it came from. To her, he was some figure on high. He was not like the rest of us. To me, he was my boss, the man down the hall from my office.

And something more that I was still trying to fully define.

"They let you out of college, and you turn into a vixen," Trin said. I rolled my eyes. "Everyone wants to know who you are. Your face was all over the news for weeks. I didn't recognize you, I mean," she paused and gestured over my clubbing choice of jean and a t-shirt, "you looked glamourous, hello."

I laughed.

"Then my mom is on the phone talking to your mom, and she says something weird. I'm thinking to myself, no way."

I froze. "My mom is talking to people about my love life?"

Trin shrugged her shoulders. The weight of the situation did not seem to affect her at all. "To my mom, but they were roommates when they were in college. Anyway, I went and pulled up one of those pictures online and I'm like 'damn.' Why didn't you tell me you were dating a billionaire?"

Someone came in and headed to the stalls. I leaned against the counter and sighed. I was going to have to talk to my mother. I thought she had the good sense to not talk about this to everyone she knew. I hoped that Trin's mother was just an exception.

"It's complicated," I said.

"I'll say. So, what's he like in bed? I was reading up on him, and apparently he likes the rough stuff."

I shook my head. "You know I don't talk about that."

Trin frowned. She took my hands and led me back out to the club. We danced for another song and then headed out to the next club on the strip. As we went in, a thick techno beat, devoid of any pop, sounded. Nina, Jakes girlfriend, began to bounce happily, as we paid our cover and made our way past the bouncers.

The music thumped and black light dominated the club. I looked around for some clue as to what was taking place tonight. This was certainly different. Usually this club was brighter and the music was loud, but more subdued with a light pop beat. Our group pushed through the crowd and Trin frowned when we found the dance floor roped off. Jake muscled through and found us a couple of high tables near the bar to gather around. He and Lewis left for drinks while the rest of us took our place on stools or standing.

From here, we had a reasonable view of the dance floor. Slowly the boys came back with drinks and we each took ours. Rum and coke. I thought to myself that the boys were going all out tonight.

"The bartender said there's some kind of fetish show," Jake said over the sound of German lyrics on an industrial beat.

My friends shrugged, but I was intrigued. I indicated that I wanted to wait, and everyone nodded or shrugged their acquiescence. After another song, the music volume decreased and two people walked out onto the dance floor. A woman in stiletto boots led a man on a leash. Around us, people whistled. I tried to focus on them.

The woman stopped and barked an order that I could not hear over the crowd. That he could amazed me. Perhaps the routine was rehearsed, orders memorized like lines. He lowered himself to his hands and knees. The woman raised her leg and placed her foot on his ass, letting the heel dig into the vinyl pants he wore. She held up a flogger, presenting it to the crowd, who cheered for her to smack him. She brought it down swiftly on his ass, and the snap of the tails reverberated over the crowd.

"Now that's what I call pussy whipped," Lewis said. He laughed as Jake shoved his shoulder for the awful joke.

I just rolled my eyes. Around me, my friends cracked jokes about the show. I was entranced with the artful way the Dominatrix moved. She stepped around her submissive in careful steps, striking at his buttocks and thighs. When she was done with the flogger, she pulled his hair, forcing his mouth open. She placed the handle in his mouth and let him go. She pulled another whip from her belt, this a two-pronged beast that made me flinch to see it. When she struck him with it, his grunt through the handle of the flogger was loud enough for me to hear.

Jake made another joke, this one getting louder laughs. I thought about who was missing from our crowd tonight. I had been agonizing over how my friends were drifting away into new lives. I realized now that I was drifting too. Listening to them crack jokes and jeer, I understood what I did not want to admit before. I did not tell my friends about Henry and me. It was not because of how complicated the relationship was. It was simply because I knew that they would not understand. None of us got into kink in college. The closest we got was body shots in Panama City.

I was entering a world that they did not understand or respect. It bothered me, and I did my best to mask the effect of their jeers. These people were professionals, opening a part of themselves to the general public. My friends mocked this, not knowing that in a way, they mocked me as well.

After the show ended, the dance floor was cleared of sweat and opened. We danced for a couple of songs, but I was not feeling it. I wanted to get out of the club. I started out, and my friends followed, probably assuming it was just time to move to the next. We squeezed through the crowd and out to the street.

"Hey, it's the freak show," Lewis pointed up the sidewalk.

I turned to see the fetishists loading equipment into a van. They must have just finished unwinding. I wondered if they would be moving on to another club or retiring for the evening.

"Hey, sweetie," Lewis called out to the Dominatrix as she walked to the van. She leaned in next to another woman who was testing equipment and deposited a small crate. "Come here if you want to see a real man."

"Can it Lewis," I said. I was growing impatient with his immaturity. "You don't get it, just deal, and move on."

The woman testing equipment turned and my blood froze. I had not seen her in the demonstration or in the club. Had she been in the background, or simply somewhere else? She put down the rope she was inspecting and walked toward us. Lewis backed away. Even he could sense that she was not someone to be trifled with.

"I suppose that you do get it then, Miss Stacy?" Mistress Aevia's voice was cool, even and full of mockery.

"Yes, I do." I turned to my friends. "Go on to the next club. I'll catch up."

Reluctantly, they turned and walked on. They could sense drama, but I did not want them to witness this. I turned back to Mistress Aevia and met her gaze. We were not at a party or an event. Here, she was a person, just like me.

"What is your problem with me?" I asked, doing my best to keep my gaze steady. She was an intimidating and imposing woman.

"You are trouble," Mistress Aevia said. "Plain and simple and trouble. I have seen a hundred women like you come through the scene in the past few years. I call you Midnight Submissives. You are oh so willing to do anything under the covers and behind closed doors. But to you it is just a game. You are not serious about your submission, you don't understand what is behind it. You are fake."

I gritted my teeth. I wondered how much of this poison she fed to Henry and wondered if it was beginning to sink in to him. Was that, then, why he did not push for more, or why he still kept me at arm's length in some ways? Were her words starting to get to him?

"You know nothing about me," I said. "And it doesn't matter. *You* don't matter." Her eyes darkened. I steeled myself and continued. "The only person who matters is Henry."

"Nice words. They convinced him. They don't convince me. You waltzed into his life with your baggage. You started trouble, and you will waltz back out again." Mistress Aevia stepped closer to me, so that I had to tilt my head to look up at her. From the corner of my eye, I could see the others and thought I saw sympathy there. "Henry can handle a lawsuit. He can probably even come out of it all with his reputation in tact. He won't be so lucky when you show your true colors. He will finally see you for what you are, and once again, he is going to be left heartbroken and bleeding. Another pretender, thinking she can be a submissive. Do you know who will be there to pick up the pieces and put him back together again? I will."

I kept myself steady, but questions began to flood my mind. I started to wonder if my assumption that Mistress Aevia was his obsession was actually true. If that obsession had been a submissive, one he trained and collared, who was only playing at her submission before turning and walking out, then so much about him made sense.

I averted my eyes in my thoughts, and realized my mistake too late. When I looked back, Mistress Aevia was leaning closer, mistaking my action for deception.

"This time," she said. "This time I will make sure Henry sees you for what you are. I will not let another little bitch break his heart."

Mistress Aevia turned and walked away. I stared after her, seeing the sympathetic looks from the others, but not really processing them. I backed away slowly, my mind spinning with thoughts. Was this all just a game after all? No, I knew better. I felt the depth of my submission already. I knew I craved to give him more. I thought about Michael and how I was managing, barely, to keep him at arm's length. How did that look? How much had Mistress Aevia already poisoned Henry's mind with her assumptions about me? How much had I contributed to it, not even realizing what I was doing?

I turned and walked down the strip to the next club. My mind burned with questions, and I no longer wanted to be here. I thought of strong arms, ropes around my wrists, and thought that I have never wanted to be with Henry as badly as I wanted to now.

THE END

Thanks for Reading!

I hope you enjoyed reading Broken Purity. ☺

Make sure you get a copy of the next book in the Alpha Billionaire Series Book 3: Broken Chasity

I would be so grateful if you please leave me a review ☺. I would love to get your feedback.

You can leave me a review by <u>clicking here</u>.

A new series will be coming up soon. And you never know Henry and Stacey may be back again!

Sign up to my mailing list below to be the first to be notified of the release of my next book coming out shortly! ☺

Also when you sign-up please feel free to send me an e-mail with your opinion and suggestions. I would love to hear from you!

Just go to www.BridgetTaylor.Info to sign up

*EXCLUSIVE UPDATES

*FREE BOOKS

*NEW REALEASE ANNOUCEMENTS BEFORE ANYONE ELSE   GETS THEM

*DISCOUNTS

*GIVEAWAYS

FOR NOTIFACTIONS OF MY _NEW RELEASES_ :

Never miss my next FREE PROMO, my next NEW RELEASE or a GIVEAWAY!

SIGN UP TO RECEIVE A FREE BOOK, BONUS CHAPTERS AND THE LATEST RELEASES:

Just go to www.BridgetTaylor.Info to sign up

43928081R00060

Made in the USA
San Bernardino, CA
07 January 2017